To Ben, my pants-tastic illustrator ~ C. F.

For Ruth, with all my love ~ B. C.

ALADDIN

An imprint of Simon & Schuster Children's Publishing Division

1230 Avenue of the Americas, New York, NY 10020

First Aladdin hardcover edition October 2011

Text copyright © 2010 by Claire Freedman

Illustrations copyright © 2010 by Ben Cort

Originally published in Great Britain in 2010 by Simon & Schuster UK Ltd.

For information about special discounts for bulk purchases,

please contact Simon & Schuster Special Sales at 1-866-506-1949 or business@simonandschuster.com.

The Simon & Schuster Speakers Bureau can bring authors to your live event.

For more information or to book an event contact the Simon & Schuster Speakers Bureau at

1-866-248-3049 or visit our website at www.simonspeakers.com.

Manufactured in China 0711 TOP

2 4 6 8 10 9 7 5 3 1

Full CIP data for this book is available from the Library of Congress.

ISBN 978-1-4424-2830-0

ISBN 978-1-4424-3576-6 (eBook)

Aliens Love Panta Claus

ILLUSTRATED BY
Ben Cort

CLAIRE FREEDMAN

aladdin

NEW YORK   LONDON   TORONTO   SYDNEY

The aliens are excited,
As tomorrow's Christmas Day.
So instead of stealing underpants,
They're giving them away!

They jump into their spaceships—whee!
And whizz off to Lapland,
Full of the Christmas spirit,
To give Santa Claus a hand.

The aliens read the letters
from all the girls and boys.
And, just for fun, they add a pair
of pants in with their toys!

In Santa's busy workshop
they cause lots of jolly snickers,
When dressing up the little elves
in fancy, frilly knickers.

The reindeer wear their underpants
    lit up all bright and glowing.
With neon pants to light the way,
It helps show where they're going!

Great! Santa's nearly ready,
But when he turns his back,
The aliens swap a spotted pair
of undies for his sack!

"Ho-ho-ho!" laughs Santa,
But his smile turns to a frown.
He won't be going anywhere.
His sleigh has broken down!

It's aliens to the rescue,
With their spaceship for a sleigh.
So reindeer bells a-jingling,
Here comes Panta Claus—
hooray!

They hover over rooftops,
And it really is fantastic.
How Santa shoots down chimneys
on a rope of pants elastic!

The aliens follow Santa
as he tiptoes to each bed.
They take down all the stockings
and tie up underwear instead.

They decorate our Christmas trees
with festive undies cheer,
And leave out underpants that say,
"An alien woz 'ere!"

An alien woz 'ere!

Then, mission done, they fly back home
to plan their next attack.
So hold on to your underpants.
The aliens **will** be back!